Pearls...

E. Hughes

Love-Love Publishing – Madison, WI
Paperback ISBN: 978-1-961823-03-7
Hardcover ISBN: 978-0-997320-02-2
eBook ISBN: 9781733445450
Title: *Pearls...* | E. Hughes
Digital distribution, 2023
Paperback edition, 2023
Hardcover edition 2023
Third edition

iii

Preface

"*Pearls...*" is a collection of stories about a handful of women, the karmic sum of their actions, and the Seven Deadly Sins of Life.

-   E. Hughes

I wrote *Pearls...* when I was in college in 1999 with some of the stories written in dialect. The stories won first place in the college's first annual English Writing Contest. That year, I was inspired by Maya Angelou, who was the keynote speaker at a different college, Chicago State University's annual writer's conference on October 23, 1999 in Chicago, IL where I also attended the event. I also saw the great Gwendolyn Brooks that day, and many other noted literary writers of that time. Inspired by some of the great literary authors and speakers in attendance, my writings would soon evolve that year from screenplays and poetry, to short stories, and less than a decade later, to fiction novels and eventually non-fiction and children's books. Thank you for reading. I hope you enjoy *Pearls....*

Other novels and works by E. Hughes:

Nonfiction
Reality Unbound: The Digital Mind (and the nature of reality) - Philosophy
Time and the Multi-Universe: A philosophy of time and time travel - Philosophy
Starting Your First Potted Vegetable Garden

Fiction:
Sixth Iteration
Disappear, Love
Business as Usual
A Mediterranean Romance: The Capa Royals
The Sapphire Chronicles: Broken Lair
Infatuation
Space, Time, and Loneliness (A Poetry Chapbook)
Beyond the Plain (Poetry)
Digital Smiles (Poetry)

Children's Books:
Penelope Helps Mom and Dad
Penelope: Be Kind to Animals
Penelope: Super Duper Spectacular Princess Ballerina
Penelope: Don't be Afraid
Penelope: Holiday Cheer
Kissing Henry (Young Teen)

The Pearls

Pearls...

When his hand slapped my face it felt like I had been hit with a hot shovel. I saw a blinding light. I fell to my knees and looked up at him. He faded in. A towering menace glowering down at me, staring into my eyes as if I had just opened Pandora's Box and was the reason his life and the rest of the world was so miserable. I knew instinctively what to do next.

With my shoulders slumped over, I slid as gracefully as I could to my knee. It was hard trying to get back on my feet without stumbling in three inch heels. But I needed to look graceful. He would have mercy on me then.

The steak was medium rare, the way he usually took it. But tonight he wanted it well done. A friend at work told him he could get some disease from uncooked meat. When he cut into his steak and saw red juices spilling from the center, without any warning he hit me hard. He hit me so hard I tasted blood at the back of my mouth. I swallowed it.

I walked to the kitchen sink. My vision was still trying to get back to normal. "-I, -I'll put this back in the oven," I stammered.

"Never mind." He cut into the steak like it was the best thing he ever ate, only seconds after hitting me across the face and accusing me of trying to kill him with it. Meanwhile, I pretended the fight never happened.

"Sit down," he demanded while staring at me.

I sat in the seat opposite of him and cut into my steak. It was well done just the way I liked it.

He stared at me as I cut the meat into neat little squares. "I see you got yours nice and done."

I smiled, pretending we were having a normal husband-wife conversation. He cut me down with one look. The inside of my stomach lurched as I prepared myself for what might be another blow. But instead of hitting me, he pushed his plate over to my side of the table then snatched mine from in front of me.

"Eat it."

I was confused. I stared at the medium- rare steak. He didn't cut his into neat little pieces like I did. He picked the entire thing up with his fork and bit into it with his teeth and ripped it apart like a lion stripping away the legs of a gazelle with its teeth. The edges of his steak looked well chewed. I could also see bits of rice stuck to it... rice from unbrushed teeth.

"I didn't hear you," I stammered, unsure of how I was supposed to respond to his demand.

He hit the side of my head with his palm.

"You hear me now?"

I nodded.

"Eat it," he said staring at me.

"You want me to eat your food?"

"What's the matter? It's not poisoned is it?"

"No."

"Then eat it."

He took my plate away and started eating the neatly cut pieces of meat. I stared down at the mangled steak on my plate. I wanted to vomit.

"Go on, eat it," he repeated.

I took a knife to the steak and cut it into pieces. He smiled, seemingly amused by what he could frighten me into doing.

I ate the steak then cleared the table when he was done. "Do something about that face of yours."

I left and went into the bathroom. There was a bruise on my cheek. I was used to those.

I took a little flesh colored makeup and covered the darkening mark. But nothing could hide the scars and bruises he left on the inside, deep where my heart used to be.

I waited until I heard the sound of his chair scraping across the floor as he made his way from the table to the kitchen. I tried to sneak upstairs before he would make his next demand. But he was hot on my heels. I was only half way up when I felt his hand digging into my shoulder. I turned around, unsure of what he wanted next.

"What in the hell is that?" he asked, staring at me with an angry look on his face.

"What is *what*?" I murmured, hoping my vacant response wouldn't tick him off. Sometimes, he would hit me if I acted like I didn't know what he was thinking, like I could read his mind or something.

"These got' damn pearls," he said, running his hand along the nape of my neck.

I was relieved.

"Oh, these," I said with a smile on my face. "I bought them from the drug store. They were only a dollar. I thought they looked pretty so I bought them. I bought them to look pretty for you," I explained, hoping my devotion would cheer him up.

"Did I tell you to buy some got' damn pearls?"

I shook my head.

"Do you do anything without me telling you to do it first?"

I shook my head then waited. He let me go.

"Don't run off. Katie and Trapper are coming over."

"Okay."

"WHAT?"

I slunk down, twisting my head to the side to avoid the fist sure to come swinging at me.

"I meant, yes, thanks for letting me know."

He sat on the couch and I let out a sigh of relief. About an hour later Katie and Trapper came by. Why he insisted on inviting them over was beyond me. Katie was a wild child and Trapper was a cuckold who worshiped the ground she walked on. We had nothing in common. When they stopped by I served drinks and spoke only when spoken to.

I answered the door when Trapper arrived, careful to avoid the friendly hug he offered. He gave me a strange look, came in and took his muddy boots off, handing me the yellow trucker hat he wore on his head. I hung it on the coat rack. Katie wore a miniskirt, a halter top, and a pair of cowboy boots. Katie and Trapper moved to the sofa feeling each other up as they sat down. But I could tell Trapper was here on business. He was still wearing his dirty work clothes.

Katie plopped down on the cushion beside me, smiling in my face as she popped the gum in her mouth. Ash would never let me behave like that. Not in public or private.

"Sowhatcha doin'?" Katie asked.

Ash glared at me. "Not a got' damn thing," he answered. "Upstairs watching television. Soaps before you got here."

Katie rolled her eyes. "Can't she answer herself?"

"Baby you know better than that. It's not our business," Trapper answered nervously.

Ash gave his friend a dangerous look.

"Put that dog of yours on a leash Trapper."

Katie jumped up. "You're a real asshole."

Ash turned and glared at me, like it was my fault...like I said something to them about the beatings. I pretended not to hear them.

"Don't worry about us. We're not staying long," Trapper said.

"Good," Ash replied, slurping the foam off the top of his beer can.

"Just stopped by to let you know we're gonna drill the entire walkway tomorrow. So make sure you got all of your equipment."

"I got the blueprints from John this morning. I'm making some changes tonight then we're good to go."

Trapper stood then hastily moved toward the door. I gave him the yellow trucker hat.

"All right, Well I'm gonna go home and get showered. We're going out tonight," Trapper smiled.

"Sure is. We're going to that new steakhouse down the road then off to the bar for some dancing!"

Katie squealed, spun around, then pulled up her skirt in an act of defiance and flashed her damn-near naked ass at Ash.

He turned red, a vein throbbing on the side of his temple. For a second, he looked like his eyes were about to pop out of his head. Trapper slid between him and Katie, blocking the view. The young woman giggled and nudged him in the side.

"You so jealous!"

"I'm not jealous," he shot back. "You actin' a damn fool."

Ash waved him off. "I'll walk you out."

He stood and walked Katie and Trapper to the door.

When the door closed behind them I got up, hoping he wouldn't notice me. But before I could make it out of the room, Ash was calling after me.

"You tired?"

"Just a little sleepy. Can I get you anything?"

I saw him looking at the pearls.

"Don't go to bed just yet. I might need a beer or somethin'."

"Yes, honey." I hurried up the stairs. True to his word, an hour or so later he called for a beer. And when I walked in the living room I found him staring at the TV. Home shopping was on. A show he never watched. Ash was thinking about something and whatever it was, it was bothering him.

I walked out of the kitchen with a cold beer in my hand. As I got closer to him, I saw his eyes fall to the pearls on my neck again. I scurried upstairs to gather the laundry wondering if Ash wanted another beer. He could drink an entire six pack. The most it would do is make him very sleepy. I was fine with that. I looked forward to Ash getting drunk because he'd fall asleep on the couch which meant I wouldn't have to worry about him getting in bed and hogging the covers all night. I could bring him his own blanket, pull the ottoman over to his feet, and cover him up. Sometimes he'd catch me taking his shoes off and find himself in the mood for love making. He'd pull me onto his lap, raise my skirt, then pull my panties down...rubbing his five o' clock shadow across my face. It would feel like gravel. Or sand paper.

Determined to turn in early for the night, I went down stairs to fetch another can of beer for

Ash. The can he'd been drinking earlier sat crushed on the coffee table, like he'd smashed it with his fist in anger. He looked up at me as I handed the cold can of beer to him. Something seemed to catch his eye. At first I thought he was looking into my blouse. It fell open, showing my breasts, which hung like pears when I bent over. I could see them as I followed his eyes to my neck area. That's when I realized he wasn't looking at me. He was looking at the pearls.

I stood upright, preparing to walk away, but he got up and followed me. I braced myself.

"You want to tell me why you really bought them pearls?"

"I told you earlier. I wanted to look pretty. For you."

"You sure about that?"

"Of course, I love you. I want to make you happy." I wasn't lying. He'd beat me harder if I looked disheveled.

"You sure you not trying to look good for that asshole from down the street? Did he buy you these pearls?"

I had to think. What asshole? Down what street? I blinked.

Ash slapped me hard and ripped the pearls from my neck. I fell to the floor at his feet. I could see the beads rolling across the hardwood floor. A few of them continued towards the dining room, and under the couch. Ash's foot came crunching down on one as he walked toward me, causing him to nearly slip and fall. That pissed him off even more. With two large steps he was standing over me. He lowered one of his boots to my face and stepped lightly on my cheek like he was crushing a bug.

"Answer me," he demanded.

I shivered. Then I remembered. One night after Ash had beaten me, I stumbled out of the house, wandering down the street in my nightgown. One of our neighbors found me and kindly took me home.

When Ash opened the door and saw me standing there with Mr. Moore, a strapping distinguished type in his late forties, his mouth dropped. He didn't even know I was gone. Ash never let me forget about that. He was obsessed with it. After Mr. Moore left me there, Ash pulled me inside and beat me some more. I woke up in the hospital that time.

Ash pressed his dirty boot down onto my face. I swallowed hard. I couldn't feel my own tongue and saliva spilled out of my mouth onto the floor.

"-No. I bought them for you," I said.

Ash took his boot off of my face then kicked me in the mouth. My head went back and banged into the coffee table.

"You left this house in your damn drawers because you wanted him to fuck you. You filthy slut. I know what you want. Think you can get me drunk so you sneak out to be with him. Right? Huh bitch? Huh slut? Well guess what? You're my whore. Nobody else's."

He grabbed me by the hair. Blood ran down my chin and my eyes rolled to the back of my head. He ripped my blouse off, slapped me across the face with it, then slammed me into a nearby wall.

Then it was over. He walked away. But I knew he'd come back to beat me some more. So I scrambled to my feet and tried to run. The room spun. I could see the door but every time I thought I was close to it, I would end up somewhere else. Everything was one big blur, slowly coming into focus.

By the time I found the way out, Ash had returned. From the side of my eye, I could see a shiny steel object in his hand. Was it a knife?

I turned and looked when his hand locked on to my neck. He gripped the shiny object with his other hand, and was coming directly towards me with a pair of scissors. Was he going to cut me? I tried to pull away, backing into a wall. I looked up, vision still blurred. That's when I realized he was cutting my hair.

I had long chocolate brown hair that I wore pulled back into a ponytail. Ash used to love my hair. He would run his fingers through it back when we were in college and tell me how beautiful it was. He would tell me that he loved my almond shaped eyes and the way my hair fell against my mocha colored skin. And now he was cutting it.

Chunks of my hair fell to the floor in bundles. After all of it was gone, and I was bald enough for him, he spun me around and pushed me against our big oak coffee table. He ripped my skirt off first, then my underwear. I looked up and saw him behind me. There was a big mirror in a gold colored frame right in front of my face. I looked at myself. All of my hair was gone. He used the scissors to give me a splotchy looking buzz cut.

I gripped the sides of the coffee table and scratched the edges of the finish away with my finger nails as he entered me. He wanted me to scream in pain. Instead, I watched him through the mirror. Not flinching or batting an eyelash. Blood spilled out of my mouth. My eyes were blackened, my tooth was chipped, and there he was, banging me from behind, grunting loudly with every thrust.

I watched him in the mirror like a woman jailed and the only freedom I could find was through the mirror...through the strength in my own eyes. I used to pity the girl I saw in the mirror, but no more. I gripped the coffee table feeling stronger as I clinched as hard as I could trying to force him out of me.

At first he looked surprised, then shivered with orgasmic satisfaction. I felt a warm rush of liquid enter me. A few seconds later it turned cold and slimy. At last, the ordeal was over.

I was still holding the table as he moved away. I watched him through our reflections in the mirror. He could barely make eye contact with me as he zipped his pants and walked out of the room. I bent over, naked and hurting inside, Ash's essence streaming down my inner thighs. It smelled just like him.

Rank. Like fish.

I didn't curl into a ball like I usually would after a beating. And he didn't slap me down for being on my feet like he normally would if I tried to get up. Instead, he stood in the doorway and watched as I collected my chocolate brown locks from the floor.

I met his eyes, glaring at him as I walked away and went upstairs. Slow. One stair at a time...the impact of my weight crushing the carpet beneath my feet. I didn't tip toe softly by. My shoulders did not slump.

I went to the bathroom first and stood in front of the mirror admiring my new buzz cut and newly chipped tooth. I was hardcore. I could take a punch to the chin like a drunken sailor with a weekend pass. I was not fragile. I was not afraid. I braved too much for too many years to call myself afraid.

I grabbed a wash cloth, wet it with warm water then wiped my face. I rinsed it again, then wiped between my legs. I wanted his filth off of me. No time for a shower. I heard Ash knocking on the door. "Get your whore ass out of there NOW!" he demanded.

I stood there, glaring at the door. I could take anything. I was not fragile. I was not afraid. I opened the door. My eyes burned into him. He stared at me, looking at *me* for the first time not sure of who he was seeing, instead of trying to cower me into a corner where he could hit me. He moved to the side. I walked into the bedroom and closed the door.

I stayed in there for about an hour. When I came out I was wearing a t-shirt, a pair of jeans, and was carrying two suitcases. I carried one in my hand, the other I had slid up my arm.

I felt strong. I carried the two suitcases with one arm while hiding my other hand behind my back. Then I walked down the stairs.

Ash was lounging on the couch. One hand on his crotch, the other on a can of beer. He looked me up and down, staring at me as if I had lost my fool mind.

"What in the fuck do you think you're doing?"

I walked past him. He jumped up fast, making sure I didn't make it to the door. Then laughed.

"Hmph. What? You think you're leaving?"

"Get out of my way," I said quietly, voice trembling with anger. He was genuinely taken aback. Then he made the mistake of flinching.

I swung my hand from behind my back and hit him as hard as I could with one of his construction tools. It looked like a wrench, except it was bigger. And very heavy. I was surprised I could even lift it. I looked at Ash as he fell backwards holding his mouth, four of his front teeth gone. His eyes were wide open staring at me in complete and utter shock. He could do nothing but cover his mouth and try not to scream. "Tyson! What in the hell do you think you're doing?"

He bled through the fingers covering his mouth, blood spurting here and there and down his shirt. I pulled the tool back again, this time over my head. His eyes widened with fear and shock as it came down, smashing him on the shoulder and back, as he curled up, trying to protect himself from my furious blow. I could have killed him. But I didn't. I had a life to live. He stayed curled into a ball, afraid to look up as I grabbed my suitcases with two hands and walked out the door. I didn't look back.

Needless to say, Ash and I got a divorce. He tried to reconcile, but I wouldn't hear him out. Instead, I pushed for the divorce and accepted alimony. Ash had a degree in architecture and owned a construction company. I had a degree in Interior Design. A degree that I had never bothered to use until I was completely free and had become a woman in my own right.

I settled the divorce, leaving him the house and everything in it, and taking nothing with me but alimony. Money, I later used to help make a new life for myself. I now live with my lover. Tandy. A pretty black woman who will take no type of shit off of anybody, and loves pearls. We play together, sometimes a little roughly. But Tandy doesn't mind. She's a strong woman, but feminine and beautiful at the same time.

By the way, I still wear my buzz cut. I also wear jeans when I'm not working. I hear Ash has a new wife and a baby on the way. I was worried at first. Then I thought about it. I suspect the wire in Ash's jaw, and six months without solid food taught him a valuable lesson.

Don't make the same mistakes me and your mother did. Love is for the birds."

Another pearl of wisdom. I called them, "Cocoa Pearls."

Pearls of Wisdom

Growing up we called her the "Diana Ross" of the hood. She was the most elegant woman I had ever seen. She was poised, sophisticated, and owned the prettiest house in our neighborhood. In fact, her house would be the prettiest no matter where she lived. She had been there long before the economic backbone of the area had checked out, and all the gangs and poor people moved in. It was like her not to move with all the so called "upper-class" folk. It was her obliviousness to change that made her this way. The world could crumble at her feet and she would still be standing there like an ancient tower. All the young people admired her. Most adults admired her too. Sometimes the kids would wave and smile when she walked out of the house to go wherever it was that women like her went. And when she smiled back the entire block lit up like northern lights.

She was all glitz and all glamour looking at me from down her perfectly shaped nose. Her name was Cocoa. Finally, after watching her for the past ten years I would be a part of her world.

I was a mere eighteen years-old when I moved in. I carried all of my worldly possessions in one plastic grocery store bag. It was small. Inside were cotton panties, two pairs of socks, a pair of blue jeans, and a bar of soap.

Cocoa looked me up and down, examining me from head to toe. I went pigeon toed when her made-up eyes landed on my flat white, rubber-bottomed, five-dollar tennis shoes. She smiled politely at the mustard stains on my jeans. Then shook her head in disapproval of my sloppy ponytail.

"I can see there's a lot of work to be done."

I was nervous. So nervous I thought I was going to pee on myself and get thrown out before I had even made it in.

"Well come on in girlfriend, make yourself at home," she said comfortably.

I walked in and she took the bag out of my hand, walked into the kitchen, and promptly tossed it in the garbage. When she returned, she sat on the edge of the couch and crossed her legs. She wasn't the thinnest woman in the world, but she wasn't fat either. She was curvy like an hourglass or a Coca-Cola bottle.

"Here are the rules. Breaking one of them will get you kicked to the sidewalk like a stray cat. Understand?"

I nodded.

"Good. The first rule is nobody touches my man. I catch you looking at him, trying to court or seduce him behind my back and I will claw your eyes out. This rule is not flexible; it is not to be negotiated, or forgiven. Rule number two... you are to be responsible around here. Pull your own weight. Since you have no money of your own just yet, you will accomplish this by cooking some of the meals, cleaning, and maintaining the overall look of the house. I guess what I'm saying is don't treat this like Cocoa's house, treat it like it's your own. We both live here now. This is *our* house. But understand something else sweetheart, I'm mama. Which means you do as I say. I won't make any out of line demands on you or anything, but I fully expect you to have some respect for whatever wisdom I have to offer. I'm fifty-five years young. I know a lot. And you're young enough to be my granddaughter. So you will treat me with the utmost respect. Get out of line, and I will crush you like a fat woman on a loaf of bread. You got me?"

I nodded.

"Good. Now I figured you're probably a size eight. So I took the liberty of picking up a few items. Good thing I did too, because you don't have much with you. Come on, let me show you to your room," she offered gently.

I followed her like a puppy trailing behind a string of sausage.

She opened my room door. There was an elegant looking canopy bed and velour burgundy colored drapes tied together with little gold ropes. There was also a vanity and a closet full of clothes. I could only imagine what her room looked like. I tried to contain myself. I was so used to sleeping on park benches I wasn't sure if I even remembered how to sleep on a bed.

"I always wanted a daughter," she said. "A daughter to share my life with, to teach... Unfortunately, I wasn't blessed like all the other women in the neighborhood who went on to have a little girl or two. Now it seems like my bad fortune has changed now that you're here. Well," she sighed. "I guess I better leave you to your own entertainment. I'll be in my bedroom. I have to take my medication. Get changed. I left something on the bed for you."

She smiled at me then walked out, closing the door behind her.

I looked around the room. This was it. This was home. I found a piece of lingerie on the bed. It was similar to the one she was wearing. Mine was cream colored, hers was black. When I walked into Cocoa's house, I was too smitten to wonder why she was wearing that black satin piece of lingerie in the middle of the day. I also wanted to ask about the medication. What kind did she need to take? And why? But she had already closed the door so I figured it was too late to ask. Maybe even a little impolite.

I went into an adjoining bathroom and took a shower, letting the warm water sort my nerves. I came out and got dressed in the satin nightie Cocoa left sitting on my bed for me. Afterwards, I left the room then tiptoed barefooted down the stairs. I could smell dinner cooking. Cocoa was in the kitchen, fully dressed, looking me up and down as I walked in.

"Melanie, can you have dinner in your room tonight? I know it's your first night here and all, but I have a gentleman caller," she smiled. "From the time to time you'll see different men folk coming through. My various boyfriends.'

She laughed, rolling her eyes into the top of her head as she fanned about.

"Which reminds me, there's a couple of other rules I forgot to mention. If anybody comes by without me telling him it's okay to come by, without invitation or phone call, he can't come in. I can't have any of my boyfriends bumping into each other. All right? Never EVER break this rule because it can cause trouble for me and I can't have anybody messing up my money. You got me girlfriend? You don't mess up my money and I won't mess up yours."

I nodded.

"Which leads me to my next rule. You are gonna have to make some friends of your own. You know what I mean by friends right? Boyfriends. You only got an eighth grade education, but you are pretty as can be. If I had your looks I'd have money comin' out the watooosy right now. But I don't. I'm older now. But the difference between me and other women my age out there struggling to make it, is that I will do what I have to do to get mine. I deserve it. Tomorrow you can go to the salon and have your hair done. On me. Then maybe we can hang out at the library or some other place where you can meet a nice older man. No sense in waiting around."

"I'm not having sex with men for money," I said, a defiant look in my eyes. I had been on the streets for too long to fall into any traps. If there was one thing I learned was how to fight for myself, and resist 'doing what I needed to do' especially when it came to sleeping with men.

Cocoa gave me a disappointed look, slipped an oven mitten on her hand, then took some bread buns from out of the oven. "Child, you got a lot to learn," she said, sounding annoyed.

"What's that supposed to mean?"

"Exactly what it does. You got a lot to learn. Who said anything about sleeping with men for money? Do I look like a pimp to you?"

"No."

"Then why would you even fix your lips to say something like that to me?" she said, smacking her mouth indignantly while fanning the bread buns so that they'd cool faster. "The second you lay down with a man you can pretty much forget about getting any money out of him."

A pearl of wisdom. Cocoa turned her back on me, puttering around the kitchen like I wasn't there.

"And where's your mama? Did she teach you anything about men? 'Bout life? You don't seem to know much," Cocoa absent-absentmindedly added. She opened a pot on the stove and sprinkled in some seasoning.

"Everything I know I learned from the streets. I ain't seen my mama since I was thirteen."

"I use to go high school with your mama."
Cocoa stirred the food in the pot, then turned the
fire down.

"She never told me that."

"She probably don't remember... her mind
being gone because of those drugs and all. Poor
Coral. She was a beautiful woman. Intelligent
too. Could have had or been anything she
wanted. "

I got quiet. I wasn't sure if I knew how to talk
about my mama yet. Especially in front of
Cocoa. Sadness threatened to overwhelm me so I
stood there staring at her... stone-faced. I was a
pro at concealing my emotions particularly
when I felt most vulnerable. And I guess it must
have showed because Cocoa took one look at me
then came around counter and gave me a hug.

"I want you to remember something
sweetheart, your mother loves you. She truly
does. She just didn't know *how* to love you. She's
sick. Sick from years of drugs abuse. It was the
poison running through her veins killing her
mentally. And baby, it is a slow agonizing death.
She had to get away. So don't go blaming
yourself and wondering why. If Coral was in her
right mind she would have given you
everything she had. Those drugs took her
soul...poor Coral."

Cocoa took the oven mittens off then threw them on the counter top.

"Anyway, I didn't mean to lecture. There's just, a lot of sadness in your eyes, and I hate to see that. So I tell you what I'll do. Later tonight I'll stop by your bedroom and I'll share my old high school yearbook, some photos, and some of my memories of your mother with you. How 'bout that?"

I smiled, feeling a little better. Maybe, seeing pictures of my mother acting like a normal person would help me feel better. Cocoa was still holding me by the arms, looking into my eyes as she waited for me to respond. The doorbell rang. "Oh dear, looks like my boyfriend is here. Make yourself a plate and run along. I got things to do." Cocoa left.

I made a plate then went to my room. In twenty-four hours I went from sleeping on a park bench to having everything I needed within reach. Whatever I wanted to eat, drink, or wear. The closet in my bedroom was full of designer clothes. I tried them on, spinning around before a full length mirror like a little girl playing dress up in her mother's closet. Then suddenly I was on beat, jamming to the soft jazz song floating upstairs to my ears.

I left the room, kneeling down a bit so I couldn't be seen as I peeked over the top of the staircase. Cocoa and some man who looked like he couldn't be any more than thirty, were sitting on the sofa. She had her feet folded beneath her, her eyes barely opened as he leaned over and whispered in her ear, fingers caressing her neck. Cocoa laughed out loud at whatever he said. I watched her turn her lips the other way when he moved to kiss her on the lips, his mouth landing on her cheek. She was going to make him work for whatever it was he was after.

On the coffee table there was a single red rose with a white envelope attached to it.

I went back to my room. I hoped at her age, I could hold the attention of a man twenty-five years my junior. She dressed the way girls my age dressed and took very good care of herself. She told me the secret to her youthful glow was staying out of the sun. She only ventured outside of the house at night. Even when she worked on her garden.

That was the way things went night after night. Jerry, Alan, Roberto, John, Elroy, and Mike all came over at various times. Elroy came by on Tuesday. He was Cocoa's favorite.

Whenever Elroy visited she was so happy. She made the biggest fuss over that man, and he pampered her just as much as she pampered him. Watching them together was like watching a pair of teenagers falling in love for the first time. *But don't tell Cocoa I said that!* On Elroy's day, he took her shopping and out to brunch. Sometimes they would see a movie, or come to the house and play cards and have a good time. Though sometimes, I'd catch them walking to her bedroom, Cocoa's hand behind her, his fingers reaching playfully to the small of her back. There wasn't as much hanky-panky as one would expect. And I was sometimes invited to spend time with them, like when Cocoa cooked dinner. Elroy loved Cocoa. And she genuinely loved him. But that didn't stop her from seeing the other men. On Sundays Cocoa went to church with Jerry and his two kids. Then afterwards they would go to some club and play golf. On Fridays she went to some after-hours club where she sat in the VIP section with John, a loud talking sports agent. Then on Saturdays, Alan would come over for dinner and spend the night. She was sure to send him on his way before eight on Sunday morning.

Mike and Roberto got in whenever they could fit in.

The men spent a great deal of money on Cocoa, each one, serving their own purpose in her life. Elroy paid the mortgage. Alan, her thirty year-old, paid some of the other heftier bills, including the note on the luxury Buick she drove. The bastard, actually felt entitled to stay over at Cocoa's house and was the only boyfriend she had that crossed the line every now and then.

Her other boyfriends covered luxuries like clothes and vacations. Cocoa's only legitimate source of income came from her monthly disability checks, which wasn't a lot of money and certainly wouldn't maintain the lifestyle she had grown accustomed to living. I doubt any of her boyfriends knew about the other expenses she had and how she paid for them

Aside from running here and there with all of her boyfriends, Cocoa spent time in the garden or in bed reading fashion magazines with various crèmes on her face. We never ate in the dining room. She'd eat in my room or I'd eat in hers. We'd gossip about men, talk about the bills, fashion, and the uselessness of love. Cocoa did most of the talking. She was very practical in her approach to life. I would listen to her, collecting her pearls of wisdom.

Usually about an hour before one of her boyfriends would come over, she'd take a shower, then get ready for her date. After a few weeks of living in Cocoa's house, I had grown accustomed to wearing lingerie in the middle of the afternoon. Maintaining my overall appearance for twenty for hours a day, had slowly become the norm. I'd wait until Cocoa finished reading Vogue or some other magazine, then I'd slip into her room and read the latest fashion and beauty tips. Cocoa didn't mind. I was her protégé. The more I grew to be like her, the prouder she was of me. No one had ever been proud of me before.

I pulled my share of the housework and even contemplated getting a job. But I didn't have a man, and Cocoa didn't play that. She never complained or said anything. But I knew she wanted me to get some money and soon. Not for her sake, but for my own.

Cocoa spent a week organizing a party at her house. I wondered how it would work out, with her many boyfriends and all. She said none of them knew about each other so none of them were invited. Save for John, who not only showed up, but invited some of his rich athlete friends. Cocoa said it was my "coming out" party. That night, she introduced me to some fellas. They gave me business cards or little scraps of paper with their phone numbers on them. That was how I met Eli. Eli was handsome. He was also a sports doctor who worked at the Memorial hospital. He was a smart man who graduated from an Ivy league college then went on to attend a prestigious medical school. He was forty-two years young but too old for me. I was only eighteen. But Cocoa told me not to let his age be a bother and to go get my "groove on."

Eli didn't have time for a relationship. He was looking for a woman he could spend time with between shifts at the hospital.

You know how doctors are supposed to be a good catch and all? Cocoa said if I made it too easy for him, I wouldn't get anything out of the man.

That weekend we went on our first date and were having a good time until he realized I wasn't legally old enough to drink. He "supposedly" didn't know I was eighteen years old when we met at the party. And when his eyes weren't wandering to my breast or my legs, he did his best to look disappointed for most of the night while being very careful not to cross whatever imaginary boundaries that were supposed to be in place between an eighteen year-old and a man his age. Under normal circumstances I could have cared less. But I hated the idea of disappointing Cocoa. I lacked Cocoa's gift for conversation, her ability to seduce men with her smile, her eyes, and ways.

So I decided to give the only thing I had to get Eli hooked on me. When he took me home I pulled him inside of the house. "Wait," he whispered, trying not to follow me inside.

Instead, I pushed his jacket over his shoulders and pulled him in. I could feel him tense when I touched him.

"Relax," I whispered, touching his earlobe with my lips as I pushed him onto the couch.

"Melanie, I can't-"

"Why? What's wrong?" I plied, making a sad face. "Don't you want me?" I asked, sliding out of my top.

"You're just so young and I'm-"

"I like older men." I climbed on his lap in a forward sitting position and wrapped my legs around his waist to slight resistance. I could see his lips trembling in the dim light. So I grabbed his hands and led them to my breasts so he could caress them. "Touch me. It's okay. I'm legal," I said convincingly, while touching myself at the same time. Eli leaned over and grazed my nipples with his lips so gently my legs quivered. It was like he had taken a feather to my skin, his lips brushed my nipples so lightly.

"Take me upstairs," I demanded.

Eli stood, with my legs still wrapped around his waist as carried me upstairs. I pulled him close, my arms encircling his neck. I could feel the muscles of his back under my hands. He was so strong, so virile...*soooo* powerful.

We went to my bedroom and he plopped me down on the bed. He threw his shirt off quickly, unbuckled his pants, then dropped them to the floor. Afterwards, he lifted my legs high and slid my skirt down to my ankles. I saw it go flying across room. My panties soon followed. I watched his lithe body slide into bed over mine, his penis erect and swinging, large and all too intimidating for an eighteen year-old virgin. It was the first time I had seen a man's private up close. And soon, I was the one who was on edge.

Eli kissed me. He caressed my body, leaving no place untouched. Then finally he laid his head next to mine and reached down. I could feel him tinkering around with his penis while trying to find the right place to put it.

"Not there!!" I yelled when he pressed me in the wrong place. I heard him quietly laugh.

I could feel his face smiling because we were cheek to cheek. Then I felt his penis bouncing back and forth as he tried to push it into my vagina. And even with the pressure of his penis squeezing inside of me being as painful as it was, I was determined to play it cool. He already had reservations about my age. Telling him I was a virgin would ruin the whole thing. So I bit my bottom lip and closed my eyes. I knew enough about sex to know the painful part would be over soon. But about halfway in he stopped, propped himself up on his elbows, then looked at me. "You're still a virgin," he said in a very matter-of-fact tone.

"Not anymore," I retorted.

Eli tried to get up but I wrapped my arms around his waist.

"I can't do this. It's wrong," he said.

"Pleeeeease," I cooed. "I want you to teach me. *You* Eli." It was all I had to say. Without any other reservations, he brought his face close to mine and bit my lower lip, and before I could protest he had pushed his penis all the way in. Soon, the hard part was over and we had gotten to the pleasure.

About one that morning we could hear jazz playing downstairs. Cocoa had company. So did I. I smiled to myself, feeling very grown up for the first time. Soon I was fast asleep, with Eli by my side.

Two hours later the jazz was playing again, only loudly as if to drown something out. I woke up to find Eli staring at the ceiling. Then I could hear Cocoa and a voice that sounded like Alan's. They were arguing. She sounded upset, but very controlled as she always does. Alan on the other hand was screaming at the top of his lungs. Something about other men. Who else is she fucking? Who's been over here? I told Eli to chill for a minute while I went to see what was going on. I grabbed a robe and walked out of the bedroom. I knelt down then peeked over the staircase and listened to them talking. Alan was her thirty year old. Of all of her boyfriends, he was the only one having a hard time understanding the rules. Which was ironic. He was an attorney. His entire life was figuring out the rules and trying to get around them. At one time, she liked that about him. But that was changing, and fast.

"Why didn't you answer the phone Cocoa? Do I look stupid to you?"

"Right now? Yes. You're making a big deal over nothing. And I don't have time for foolishness."

"Do you think I'm playing with you?"

"No."

Cocoa lit a cigarette. Alan knocked it out of her hand. I stood up. Cocoa and I understood that if any man got out of line in our house, we'd both throw him out on his ear. Physically kicking his ass if we needed to.

"So how many are you seeing?"

"Honey, that's none of your damned business. You don't like it, you know how to find the door."

"What if I don't want to find the door? Don't you fucking understand Cocoa? I'm giving everything up for you!" he screamed, spit flying out of his mouth, nostrils flaring.

"Did I ask you to do that?"

"Dammit you didn't have to."

"But that's your choice Alan. I'm not about to change my life for you."

Alan put his hands on his hips and took a few deep breaths. Soon, his breathing was back under control. But I could tell it was hard for him to bring himself down from where he was. "I don't want you seeing other people."

"I'm fifty-five years-old Alan. This is my world. You don't get to have what you want."

Alan stood there looking at her like a spoiled brat who, despite his tantrums just couldn't get his way. Cocoa curled her legs beneath her and stared at him.

"At least not all the time... come here," she said.

Alan walked over to her, shoulders slumped, face almost in a pout. He stubbornly folded his arms. But Cocoa was as smooth as butter. She pulled him close to where she sat on the sofa. Alan kept his arms folded as she unbuckled his pants. I could hear them unzip and see her fumbling around. It only took a few seconds for his arms to fall at his sides as he threw his head back with his eyes closed. I ran into the room, fearful that he would open them and look right into my eyes.

Alan was a mystery. All I knew was that his parents didn't approve of their relationship, Cocoa being an older woman and all, and of a different background so they both kept much about each other a secret considering, none of their friends would be able to overlook some of their obvious differences. Those differences also had everything to do with Alan's inability to follow the rules.

I got back in bed with Eli, who was still staring at the ceiling. I threw my leg over his, then laid there, pretending to be asleep.

The next morning I told Cocoa about my night with Eli. She was pleased until she heard about the virginity part. She said I should have saved myself for someone I cared about. I told her I cared about Eli. I probably even loved him because he was my first. She smacked her lips.

"Girl, what do you know about love? I squandered my entire youth on love. I could have been anything a politician, a professor, a lawyer, CEO of some company. But love lost me the best years of my life. To hell with love. I'm a businesswoman. I may not have a college degree, but I managed to become C-E-O of this *pussy*. Not a lot of women, married or single can say that," she said, pointing down as if I didn't know where "pussy" was. "The life you live, as they say, may not always be your own. If it's one thing you learn from me, is that my life belongs to me, and by virtue of paying attention to everything I'm telling you child, you're life will belong to you as well. So long as you keep all this love stuff in perspective."

Cocoa smacked her lips again.

"And I don't give a damn about anybody who cares to disagree. So I suggest you save yourself some time. Don't make the same mistakes me and your mother did. Love is for the birds."

Another pearl of wisdom. I called them, *Cocoa Pearls.*

I thought about mama falling in love with a man who got her hooked on drugs. And when it was all said and done, and she was all used up, he dumped her. Maybe Cocoa was right. Maybe she was on to something. Women like us born with broken spoons in our mouths rarely found *true* love. We find broken men, with broken spirits, who leave us with broken hearts. Men who are so down on life that they can hardly find the time to love someone else. Let alone, themselves.

I spent the next few weeks calling Eli like crazy. Cocoa was right. I should have made him wait. Eli didn't take care of me the way her boyfriends took care of her. When I told Cocoa what was going on with Eli and how I couldn't get a phone call out of him, let alone any money for that matter, Cocoa looked at me in that knowing manner of hers, and said "Hmph. You better learn how to suck a good dick," then threw her head back and laughed.

Cocoa was telling me I wasn't good enough in bed, which bugged me. But I can't say I wasn't warned. Cocoa told me don't sleep around unless you get something first. I did the reverse and was paying for it.

In fact, Eli didn't even bother to send me a card, a bouquet of flowers, not even a condom wrapper. I expected to hear something. ANYTHING, but I didn't. So I called the hospital he worked at and had him paged. He took my call thinking I was one of his patients. "Eli don't you hang up on me!" I said, after a pause came when he heard my voice.

"I'm working. This is a place of business so I suggest you say whatever it is you need to say before you find yourself having a friendly conversation with a dial tone."

He was pissing me off. "Why haven't you called? I miss you."

"I'm a doctor. I'm working so much I'm sleeping at the hospital most nights. When I want to see you, I'll let you know."

"Do you really think you're in position to decide when you get to see me? What kind of bullshit is that?" I snapped.

I could hear Eli blowing air out of his mouth. "Goodbye Melanie." He hung up.

Motherfucker.

Against Cocoa's advice once again, I fucked up. I lost my cool. Cocoa said, "Never lose your cool."

I got dressed, marched out of the house and went down to the hospital. I found him in the emergency room having coffee with some of the other doctors. When I walked in his face dropped like mercury in sub-degree weather. I walked around the station, grabbed him by his ear and pulled him into the bathroom.

"So it's over? Just like that it's over?"

"Yes."

"Why? What did I do wrong?"

"I shouldn't have slept with you, Melanie. If I'd known you were a virgin before we got started I-"

"You're dumping me for being a virgin? What kind of nonsense is that? You didn't seem to mind when I was fucking your brains out."

"I'm married."

I couldn't breathe.

"I shouldn't have spent the night with you Melanie. It wasn't fair."

I thought about Cocoa. Then felt foolish.

"You have to keep seeing me."

"I'm done with this conversation," he started.

"Really? You will keep seeing me because you have no other choice."

"Don't tell me you're pregnant..."

"I'm not pregnant. But I'll tell your wife. I don't think she'll be too amused when she finds out about me."

"If you can find her, go right ahead."

Eli smirked at me in a 'double dog dare you' sort of way.

I smiled at him, turned on my heels and walked out.

I went home and when I made it to the house I found Alan parked outside staring at the door. It was Monday. It wasn't his day. So I went over to say hello, and to perhaps, get him to go away.

"Alan? Hi, what are you doing here?"

"I pay the damned bills. I'll come when I want." He looked straight through me at the door.

"Well, Cocoa's not home right now."

"I know."

"Sooo..."

"I'll be right here when she gets back."

"Do I have to call the police on you?"

"Go right ahead. I'll just show them the electric bill. And all the other bills I pay. I know the law. I'm an attorney, Melanie. Or did you forget? I can prove I live here. Can you?"

I rolled my eyes then went in the house. When I got inside I called Cocoa's cell phone and told her to have Roberto drop her off around the corner. She was thankful for the head's up. Alan was becoming a problem.

The next day was a Tuesday. That morning I went into her bedroom and found Cocoa and Alan asleep. He was snoring like a grizzly bear. Tuesday was Elroy's day. How did this happen? I'm guessing when Alan came by the night before he got Cocoa to let him stayed over. But it was already eight o' clock and Elroy was going to be there in an hour. Cocoa opened her eyes then looked at me.

She tried to slip out of bed, but Alan grabbed her arm. She put her hand to her mouth and ear in the shape of a phone. I knew that meant I would need to call Elroy and cancel. The rules were being broken.

We spent Tuesday puttering around the house. Alan stayed all that day and Cocoa sulked. He knew he was keeping her from whatever plans she had. Overall, he seemed pleased by this. He knew about the other men, there's no telling how long he had been spying. She was bored to tears. He watched the stocks most of the day, read the paper, and drank coffee. We cooked, ate, then I went to my room and tried to figure out what it was that I needed to do about Eli.

Later that night I climbed into bed with Cocoa. She was quiet, barely paying attention to her magazines.

"Alan's got to go," I said.

"I know sweetie. But he's paying most of the bills. I can't complain about that. We've been living pretty good. All the extra money's been going towards some of our luxuries. Without Alan, there'd be no more Saturday afternoon shopping sprees, or one hundred dollar face creams until I find a replacement. Certainly no more expensive lingerie, good food, and all the other things we like if I get rid of him now. Alan is executing a hostile takeover... He's becoming *C-E-O* of *MY pussy*."

"But don't you think we're getting a little *too* greedy? Forget the bills. Alan's breaking the rules. So are we if we let him stick around."

"You're right. But I can't leave him cold turkey. He might cause a problem."

"I'll step things up and replace the money Alan brings in."

"You don't have a man, and bills don't wait for nobody."

"There's Eli."

"Chile, you need to let that sleeping dog lie. I know Alan thinks paying a bill or two gives him carte blanche over the household but-"

"I'll deal with Eli. And I'll deal with him good."

"Don't do anything foolish now-"

I smiled. "I'll deal with Eli."

I slipped out of bed and went to my bedroom. Then I grabbed the white pages and called every Eli Moyer in the book. Each time, a woman would answer. I would say "Is this the home of Dr. Eli Moyer?" I didn't find any doctors but one. And when the woman on the other end of the line confirmed it was him, I told her I was one of his co-workers from down in registration and he told me I could call and pitch makeup from my Avon catalog. Mrs. Laurie Moyer had the sweetest voice. In a way I felt kinda bad. But it wasn't anything personal against her, it was her man that I was after. She gave me her address. I told her I would be coming by to showcase the selections soon, then hung up.

The very next day I went to the emergency room and found Eli getting off of his shift. He was surprised to see me but wasn't as nasty as he was the last time we talked.

I smiled at him. Then folded my hands behind my back innocently. "Hey Eli. Laurie wanted me to send you a message. She said, don't forget to pick up her blood pressure medication on your way home." I turned on my heels and walked away. Eli followed, just like I thought he would. But I didn't give him the opportunity to catch up. I walked fast, making sure to get out of the hospital so we could talk in private, or loudly if we needed to.

When I made it outside, Eli was on my heels grabbing me by the arm, dragging me to his car.

"Let me go!" I spat at him. He took me around to the passenger side, opened the door, and shoved me in.

"What kind of games are you playing? I told you it was over."

"It's not over until I say it's over."

"What do you want from me? I said I was sorry. I'm trying to move on with my life, fix my marriage. I can't see you anymore."

"I want to be with you." I answered.

"Why?"

"You don't know why a woman like me would want to be with a man like you?"

"I'm married, Melanie."

"So. I'll never tell your wife."

"Bullshit." Eli rubbed his hands over his face then buried his head into the steering wheel.

"I want to broker a deal."

Eli looked up at me. "What?"

"A deal."

"What kind of a deal?" he asked, indignantly.

I leaned across him then pulled the lever on the side of his seat. It popped and he went falling back. The seat giving way startled him, but before he could sit up and put it back in place, I had crawled onto his lap. I slid my skirt up then pulled his hands around my waist. I wasn't wearing any panties. Eli was weak. As angry as he was with me, he couldn't resist sliding his hands between my legs and feeling the warmth and the moisture between them. Whatever I had done wrong, he had already forgiven, given the right encouragement. I could feel the bulge in his pants grow. I sat directly over it. But I wouldn't move so he could unbuckle. Instead, I rolled my hips back and forth until he was desperate to enter me. I He kept going for his belt but I kept pulling his hands away. "Let's talk about our deal." I murmured into his neck, still gyrating back and forth against his manhood.

"Okay," he said, out of breath. "You play a tough game Melanie You wanna deal. Okay. Let's deal."

"You give me whatever I need."

"Okay," he answered, going for the belt again.

I pulled his hand away. "First things first. You need to understand the rules. Rule number one, When you stop by the house, you will leave an envelope on the table. We don't need to discuss what's reasonable. You have enough common sense to know what that means. You look out for me, I look out for you."

"Anything," he managed, between biting me on the chin and rubbing my breasts. Eli grabbed the back of my neck and tried to push my face into his lap, but I resisted. The agreement needed to be clear before he got anything else from me.

"I never tell your wife. You don't break our arrangement without some notice. If you're too busy to come by, call. Be considerate, be kind, we'll treat each other with respect. Got it? I want us to be friends as well as lovers."

"Okay," he begged, like a willing puppet, going for the buckle again.

"I'm going to make this worth your while. I'll be whatever you want me to be," I said, whispering in his ear.

Eli was putty in my hands.

I stuck my tongue in his mouth. My ass was in the air, pointed toward the windshield where people could see. Eli rubbed, caressed, and went for the belt buckle again.

"This is so bad," he said.

"It's our secret Eli. Your wife will never know." I felt him relax. "I'll never ask you to divorce her, I'll never be intrusive and ask you for time you don't have."

I leaned away from him and helped unbuckled his pants. Soon, the windows in the SUV were foggy, and the vehicle was rocking. It wasn't all that hard to figure out what was going on inside.

I went home with Eli and his check in my front pocket. I showed it to Cocoa. She was relieved.

"Well, looks like you graduate with honors. We have a new benefactor," she smiled before heading to her room.

That night she told Alan it was over. He didn't take it well. Cocoa was pissed about Elroy losing his day. Elroy was Cocoa's favorite. Her main man. He was a fifty eight year-old retired engineer with a couple of pensions. Cocoa liked Elroy a lot. Hell, I was sure she loved him, but would never admit it to me. *Love was for the birds.*

Alan on the other hand, fucked up because he broke the rules and Cocoa had to rearrange everybody's day that week. Which had NEVER happened before. Needless to say, her boyfriends were a bit disturbed having their routine broken like that. Jerry couldn't see her at all on Sunday.

Which meant, she was losing money because of Alan. Even if it wasn't that much.

The next day I met a new fella. He was a good looking well-bred man who worked as the vice president of an investment firm. He didn't have a lot of time, but he was single, and had enough money to spare for me. I didn't give it up on the first night like I did the first time with Eli. I knew better. Cocoa was right. I did enough to keep him desperate for more. And the more desperate I made him, the more he gave.

Richard was my Thursday. Eli was a four day a week duty that required me to visit him at the hospital for quickies in broom closets, unoccupied spaces, or bathrooms. He would call and request blow jobs and I would go to the hospital without underwear, to give him some head. I would raise my skirt, bend over and leave. Sometimes Eli would come to the house and spend the night. We'd have breakfast in bed and make love all morning. Cocoa told me to cut him down, he was getting too much time. But it was Eli's occasional relapse into feeling guilty about cheating on his wife, that made me see him more often to remind him of what he was missing if he cut me off. But things didn't go this way forever.

I met Maestro. Odd name for a twenty eight year-old Korean man who owned a chain of beauty supply outlets. Maestro was cool. He had an appreciation for all kinds of beauty and gave me stuff from overstock from his shop, and bundles of money. He convinced me to take some classes and even paid for them. I took a high school equivalency course, and a few pottery and jewelry classes. I cut Eli down to two days a week. He was unhappy not having me at his beck and call, but he was too addicted to let me go. I didn't need him anymore, so the consequences for me weren't that severe. I cut Eli loose and moved on. He wasn't happy about that either. Poor thing.

One of my favorite necklaces to make were faux pearls. I made lots of them too. Maestro was kind to me. He said as cheap as they were, they were pretty enough to put in his stores. So I made them, and he sold them for two dollars apiece.

Cocoa continued to see Alan, who continued to break the rules. Cocoa saw him more or less out of fear than she did out of necessity. Alan was a liability. He threatened to sue her.

"For what?" I asked.

"Some trumped up nonsense. I don't know what to do about him," she answered absent-mindedly.

"Well what does he want?"

"Time. A relationship."

Alan also wanted to move in, and sleep with her for free. He asked to "re-negotiate" the terms of their previous contract. He was trying to turn her CEO brand into a dollar store. The new contract included a clause that would force her to break things off with her other boyfriends. He wanted a normal relationship. Needless to say, Alan was a pest. He was beginning to bother me and he wasn't even my man. But Cocoa handled it like an old pro, saying this sort of thing happens from time to time.

One Tuesday, Alan was over early in the morning. He had stayed over from the previous night. Cocoa managed to get him to leave about eight-thirty. He had things to do that day anyway. Lawyer business I suppose. Later on, Elroy came by and Cocoa was happy to see him. They went shopping, out to brunch, then came back to the house a later in the afternoon, laughing and joking like the best of friends. I stayed in my room that day, giving them as much time alone as they needed.

That night, thinking Cocoa and Elroy was still downstairs, I went to her bedroom to fetch a magazine.

I opened the door. To my surprise, I saw Cocoa was sitting on the bed with a needle in her arm. Her eyes were closed, and her lips were dry and clasped tightly together. Elroy was giving her a hand. They were so involved in what they were doing, they didn't even know I was there. I felt blood rush to my brain as I watched them. So I ran to my room and slammed the door. Is this why Cocoa and Elroy got along as well as they did? Were they junkies? You know what they say about two addicts! They make a helluva couple.

Feeling lied to, and moving back and forth, between the past and present, two women I loved very deeply, turning out to be a huge disappointment was too much. I couldn't figure it out. Why me? I grabbed my suitcase and went to the closet and started packing. I couldn't deal with another drug addict. I watched my mother waste away and seeing Cocoa with a needle in her arm was just as devastating to me. Everything I came to know about her wasn't real. Everything she had taught me, was total bullshit. I couldn't trust her. There was nothing special about Cocoa. She wasn't elegant. She didn't have things under control. Alan himself was evidence of that.

I took my suitcases and ran down the stairs. By the time I got to the door, I was in tears and having flashbacks of my terrible childhood. I wasn't thinking about Cocoa anymore, I was seeing my mother in a drug induced haze, standing on corners not even recognizing me as I walked by on my way home from school, or walking in on her and her crackhead friends getting high, only to be met with a slap. I saw myself walking in on my mother being raped by some drug addict, and her screaming for me to get out, as he stared at me from behind her with lust in his eyes.

I couldn't see for all the tears blinding me when I pulled the door open. And for a moment, I didn't care when I saw Alan on the other side of the door about to knock. I ran past him. I ran out of the house in a tear-induced haze.

He looked over his shoulder at me as I ran away.

Then it dawned on me. I turned around, wiping my eyes with the back of my hands. Elroy was inside with Cocoa. I turned and ran back into the house. And almost immediately, I could hear them, their voices rising to a fevered pitch. I took two stairs at a time getting up to Cocoa's room.

I could hear Elroy telling Alan to leave, and Alan screaming at Cocoa, calling her names. I made it to the top of the stairs.

Alan was standing in the doorway. And I was standing behind him when I saw the gun and heard the loud boom of a single gunshot.

"I told you not to play games with me," He said, as Elroy fell to the ground.

Cocoa fell to her knees and wept. She all of a sudden looked old. Very old. Her hair seemed to turn gray right before my very eyes. I screamed.

Alan, startled by the sound of my voice turned around, his eyes glaring. I put my hands in front of me, shielding my face, as if my hands were bulletproof. But instead of shooting, he lowered his gun. He looked confused for a moment. Then walked away. He went down the stairs. A few seconds later, I heard a gunshot.

Cocoa put her hand on Elroy's chest. "Call somebody, *anybody*," she said, rocking her body back and forth.

I grabbed the phone, which sat on the nightstand next to Cocoa's bed and dialed "9-1-1." Just as the emergency operator answered the line I looked down. On the floor next to the bed was a used syringe and an empty bottle of insulin.

Things slowed down around the house. But I was still juggling relationships. I had personal luxuries to tend to. Cocoa on the other decided to settle down. Elroy left her money, a small but healthy inheritance. She was the sole beneficiary of his will. Little did I know, Elroy and Cocoa had been married for ten years but decided they were better apart. Over the years they managed to develop a friendship based on mutual respect. Cocoa loved the fact that he never forced her to settle down, which made her feel even guiltier about his death. Nevertheless, all of his pensions were hers, as well as all of his assets. After settling the will, Cocoa gardened in her free time and started living and acting the way women her age usually do.

Cocoa once said if she didn't have me, she wouldn't have anyone else, after Elroy died. She eventually talked me into going to college, but couldn't convince me to stay with one man. I was set in my ways at only nineteen years old. We lived together in her grand old house, just enjoying each other's time. She said, I kept her young on the inside, with stories about my wild youth and man juggling lifestyle. A life, I could tell she missed from time to time.

A few years later Cocoa died of complications resulting from diabetes. She always said, she had the sweetest ass in town. I miss her. She gave me so much. My life changed because of Cocoa. And hers because of me. Maybe not in a good way, I think sometimes. When I walked in on Cocoa and Elroy the day he was a shot, he was only helping her inject a dose of insulin. Sadly, she never told me about the diabetes. But I guess it's not important now.

I thought Cocoa would hate me for leaving the door open and letting Alan walk in. After all, Elroy's death was probably my fault. But instead of yelling at me and kicking me out of her life, she said it was God's way of telling her it was time to change. Elroy's pensions were left in his place to take care of her. A punishment for all she had done wrong.

It was time to "get old," Cocoa said. That's what life is. *Change.* I guess that was the last bit of knowledge whirling out there in the Universe for

Cocoa. And I'm sure there's even more out there for me.

In the end, Cocoa left me the house and all her worldly possessions.

I went from street urchin, to ghetto goddess, from ghetto goddess to professional woman in a matter of years. If it wasn't for Cocoa making sure I went to college, where would I be? Juggling men? More pearls of wisdom I suppose. Which reminds me, I still make those faux pearls for Maestro. A chain I call "*Cocoa Pearls,*" I hear they're selling like hot cakes.

"In the end all you got is love. Because love is the last thing you gonna think about and the last thing you gonna feel..."

You Can't Take It with You

Life ain't nothing but a drama, a never ending saga. Seems like somebody up there in them clouds is laughing and playing a joke on some of us. *Or maybe we jus playing' jokes on ourselves!*

Everything I lived for, was the very thing that killed me. Ain't it funny how many different endings life will bring? How some people die peacefully in they sleep, and other folks die in a hospital or nursing home all by theyselves?

Why? Seems nothing is really important when you laying in the ground beneath all that cold dirt. Material possessions ain't really important. And money sho'll nuff ain't important cause *you can't take it with you!*

In the end all you got is love. Because love is the last thing you gonna think about and the last thing you gonna feel *(trust me I know!)* Somebody up there must have been laughing pretty hard, and was playing' a cruel joke on me, and my Pearl.

I remember looking' at my baby all dressed up in her wedding gown. She was wearing a *white* wedding gown. I made her wait. Just so she could wear that fine white wedding dress. Ohhh! She looked so pretty! Furthermore, she would have looked absolutely beautiful if it wasn't for that sad look in her eyes.

Most girls cry on they wedding day. But that wasn't why my Pearl was looking so sad. She wanted to marry that boy. That boyfriend she had since she was sixteen. But you know what I told her?

"If you marry that low class bum I will tear you to pieces! You ain't welcome in my house, and I won't never see your kids!"

That sure got rid of that boy real quick. They got outta high school and thought they was gonna get married. But my Pearl likes to please her mama, so she did just like I asked her to. She gave that boy back his jacket, and his class ring, and told him to hit the dirt! She came home looking so sad too. Just like she do today. I'm gonna have a talk with my Pearl and tell her not to drop one tear on her face. All that's gon do is smear her makeup. And I don't want her brand new husband to raise that veil and look into no sad eyes and smeared eye liner! Oh no! That won't do! Cause if it was me I wouldn't wanna marry no sad looking woman. A sad, ungrateful woman. She ought to be glad she marrying Richard. He's a famous basketball player and he's on TV all the time. He got plenty of money to take care of her and give her everything she need. Oh that's right! He come from an *af-fluent* family. They RICH! And I want my baby to be well taken care of when she leave my house. So you know what I did? I walked right up to Pearl and I told her,

"Wipe that look off your face and get it together honey. You think Richard wanna marry a sad, miserable woman? Don't no man want no miserable woman! He marry you to make hisself happy, and you gonna do everything you can to make that happen! Now straighten up your face and pull it together! Your job as a wife is to make your husband happy. So stop thinking about yourself cause there ain't no "I" in a marriage that works!"

She looked at me with them sad, miserable eyes then smiled at me as bright as she could. That smile was so bright it could have lit up the room, and she said, "Sure mama. Whatever you say…"

She gathered up that long train on the back of her gown, and rose from in front of that mirror she was looking into and walked out the room. Real slow.

Dum, dum, da dum! Dum, dum, da dum! He sholl kissed his bride! And they looked so happy. But I was feeling kinda mad…You know that boy my Pearl was trying to marry? That one I made sure she dumped? You know he had the nerve to show up here? In the church! Looking at my baby with them sad eyes of his. I gave him an evil look. Cause if looks could kill that boy would be dead! I didn't want him here looking at my baby, trying to make her change her mind. He thought he was slick. Looking at Pearl from inside them tattered clothes. I didn't want my baby's n laws thinking my daughter she was into slumming with the likes of him. That would have made her not good enough for they son. After the wedding that boy even showed up for the reception! That scoundrel! Off whispering to my daughter. I wasn't scared though. That Richard and my daughter was married! It was too late for him. And he was looking down. So sad. Walking out the door looking like he was gonna kill hisself. That would have been the best thing for him to do. What good is life if you ain't got no money? Many people ask me, *"Why you so hard on that boy? He loves your Pearl!"* But see, love don't pay no bills. Love don't put no food on the tables, and love ain't gon keep my baby in the best of nothing like some cash. She wasn't raised to wash dishes, or have no job. My baby is supposed to have a husband taking care of her! All these women call theyselves goin to work. Becoming doctors, lawyers, and police officers. Them some fools! Why would anybody go out there to work when they can stay home? And I don't mean stay home and get no welfare, that ain't no fun at all! Why would anybody want to stay home for four or five hundred dollars a month? Why, by the time they pay the rent, and the electric bill, they ain't got nothing but ten or fifteen, sometimes twenty dollars to live on. I don't see how them poor fools do it. Trying to raise three, four, five, six kids on absolutely nothing! Got the whole world on they backs calling them lazy too. Why, if women wasn't taking all them jobs from men, people wouldn't have to be on no welfare. Somebody husbands should be working them jobs. I told my Pearl she betta not ever get no welfare. Welfare is for fools. Po fools! And she wasn't gon be po! AND she wasn't gonna marry that boy, with his broke ass! Let me tell you about that boy. . . .

That boy, the one who was trying to marry my Pearl, come from a lowly family. They so po they might as well be still in slavery. His mama spent her whole life working at some restaurant cleaning, and scrubbing dishes. I would come in there and she would be smiling at me. I didn't see what was so funny! She didn't have nothing to smile about. She had them wrinkled dishpan hands, and no matter how nasty you would get at her, she would always be smiling. She didn't have no reason to be happy. She was po as dirt! And that boy of hers was just as happy, with his nothing. I didn't want my Pearl to be happy with nothing. If that woman loved her son she would have given him something. But she's a fool! You know she actually bought that boy into that restaurant to work with her on the job! And even though he spent all his time working while he was liking my Pearl, he ain't never bought her nothing! Said he was saving for his future. That's the oldest line in the book if I ever heard one. I was glad after my baby got married. That boy went away quick! Left town for free hanging on the back of a train. Silly fool. Where was he going? He had nothing and he was never gonna be nothing!

My Pearl. My baby! Moved in her first house with her brand new husband! They got theyselves a mansion. His family SO RICH! I can't wait to meet them! My baby and her husband had been married for months, and you know my n laws ain't never invited me over for a meal. You would think they want to talk about grandchildren and stuff like that! But they never said a word to me at the wedding. They didn't say nothing to me at the reception at all. They just admired that white wedding dress they bought for my Pearl. They was so happy for that dress they bought! And that church that they paid for! And the reception and photography fees they covered! Its tradition for the father of the bride to pay for weddings, but Richard's parents said we betta save our money for other things! They would pay for the entire wedding!

"Thank you," I said proudly. My husband though, didn't want them to pay. He said he could afford to pay for his own daughter's wedding, he worked hard his whole life for that day, and we middle class people! He so foolish. Husband said Richard's family was looking down they nose at us.

I told him, "Don't you know how nice rich folks are? Why would they think they betta than us? We got everything we want."

It took days before I could convince him to let them pay. After husband gave in, he left out to get a drink at some bar. He wasn't gonna spend our cruise money for that wedding when Richard's people was gonna pay for it. Money make everybody happy, and if they so rich, well they just spreading the joy. My husband ain't got no class!

A few months after the wedding, as hard as I tried, I hadn't heard from my baby in a while. I heard she be hosting dinner for Richard's rich friends. They always telling him how pretty my Pearl is (*that's because she takes after me and not her daddy!*) and how he got a good wife. I was proud. Them men he be with is so proud of Richard! They say they wish they had a wife who wanted to stay home. They got them wives who like working for charities, or law firms, or into the stock trade. And my Pearl said when them women come around they don't talk to her. And she don't talk to them! Says there ain't nothing to talk about! All she do is serve them drinks, and make sure everything is running smoothly. My daughter sounded like the happiest woman in the world. Sometimes I wished I was in her shoes. Just for a day! Living in that castle Richard bought for her. I went there once and they even had a maid. But that maid didn't make me no drink. Richard said him and Pearl had guest coming over. And he wanted to make sure things was running smoothly cause his parents was gonna be there. So I gave them both a kiss on the cheek and left. Later that night, when I went home and told my husband what happened at Pearl's house. He got up and through his beer against the wall.

"Them folks think they slick! Don't you see it baby? You need to get your nose out them clouds and see those people for what they are, and stop looking at they money! Pearl ain't happy with that man of hers and I'm gonna get my baby out of there!"

"You will do no such thing!" I hollered. "Leave them alone! Pearl is a grown woman and she can take care of herself. She ain't told me she was unhappy with Richard. So mind your own business."

Husband shook his head and sat back in the recliner. He started staring at the TV like I wasn't there. I went to bed.

I stopped off at Pearl and Richard's house. And true like my husband said, Pearl wasn't happy. My baby said Richard wasn't talking to her no more, and she bored with life and him. All they do is put on fronts for people. She says her face is like porcelain for smiling so much and want to. She said she got on her porcelain mask, and it's always smiling when she ain't even happy. "Pearl, get your husband a child and all your problems will be solved. Babies solve everything! All you need to do is give him a baby and he'll turn into a loving husband again." I don't have to tell you. She did just like I asked.

The day had arrived. My Pearl at the hospital giving birth to a lil boy! I was so happy. Richard and my Pearl was doing just fine. He was happy they was gonna have that baby! Turns out, having a baby was a good idea. At first, even I was starting to have doubts, but it all worked out. Shortly after Pearl and I had that talk... Richard's parents had been trying to talk to him about divorcing my baby. Talking bout she wasn't educated enough, and why would he marry some low class woman like her!

"What do her parents do?" they said. "You mean to tell me her father is a handy man? Her mother a retired nurse? Richard! What about the family? And everything we worked for?"

Talking about we bad for their image. His mother said it right in front of my child, with no regard for her feelings! But when Pearl announced five months later that she was gonna have their precious grandbaby everything changed! Pearl was the one who was in charge. They wanted to make sure she got everything she needed cause that baby was one of them! Ha! Call me low class? I'm always ahead. Always thinking ahead! But that night I wasn't prepared for what happened next.

Husband and I were waiting to go up and see Pearl and grandchild. But when we went upstairs the nurse said, "Family only!" in that snooty voice of hers.

I was astounded. "FOOL, I am her *mother*."

"Ma'am I was given instructions not to allow anyone up here. I was told this by Mrs. Parents themselves."

I just looked at her real crazy like, because she might as well have slapped me silly.

That was the last straw for husband. We had a big blowout. We tried to call Pearl, but the hospital didn't allow no calls after ten. It was well past twelve. Husband stormed out the hospital, threw his hat on the ground and spit. He was walking so fast I could barely get up to him.

"We'll see her in the morning. Don't worry."

"I'm tired of these people! They done did everything they could to be rude to us. I tried coming over to Pearl's house and half the time I can't even get through the door!"

We got into the car.

"Pearl is a grown woman! If she wants to see us, or if you want to see her just do it at our house. Pearl is a RICH woman and they busy all the time. We just got to respect that and let her do what she needs to do!"

Husband was driving so fast I thought we was gonna crash into something. His face was red hot and he seem to shoot fire from his eyes. He pulled in front of our house and crashed the car into the garbage can, knocking trash all over the lawn. My mouth was wide open. Then he turned around and looked at me and said, "I'm leaving and I ain't never coming back."

"Why?" I said... dumbfounded. The inside of my head was spinning like one of them electric fans.

"I'm tired of you. You and your greed. I'm tired of you carrying my wallet and my balls in your purse. I wanna be happy babe. I just wanted to get married and have a family. I done spent the past thirty-something years of my life unhappy with something I should have been happy with cause I been lusting for things, and desiring for stuff I ain't never needed. We had careers, you had a good job as a midwife! You wasn't never happy. I would have been happy if you didn't make me feel so bad for not wanting more. Now you done did the same thing to our daughter. She didn't want no baby. And I don't want money hanging out my mouth when I die. I want to be simple. Live simple. I don't need these things your heart been lusting after for so long. . . you can have the house." Husband got out of the car and slammed the door. He didn't even walk inside the house to get his clothes. He just kept walking. And I ain't seen him since.

After husband left, things went downhill. After a few months, the bills started piling up. And I still hadn't seen my grandchild. Lucky for me, Pearl paid last month's mortgage. Money been real tight since husband left. I done been so used to getting stuff without thinking about it. Budgeting was hard. Husband never did buy nothing for himself. He was always saving. For when he leaves, probably. I heard he went off and found himself some older woman. He living out there in the country with her. I bet she ugly. All them buck teeth country women are ugly. Husband keeps her house up, and they just spend time and heal each other's loneliness... Or so he tells my daughter. She said he sounded quiet and wanted to talk a little more. But she didn't have much time cause the baby had to be at church for his christening and Richard's parents were waiting.

Things went on that way for quite a while. Year after year, until the baby was about three years-old. Pearl bought the baby over sometimes. I saw them every now and then. Pearl had been helping me with the bills. Thank goodness she was rich! If she hadn't been rich I wouldn't have made it without husband. That's why I was so glad I pushed her as hard as I did to be ambitious with other folk's money. Never know when a man gonna leave you. Husband could go his way, I thought. As long as

Pearl had money I didn't need him no way. *Or so I thought...*

It was baby's third birthday. Pearl told me it was gonna be a birthday party. Still, no invitation. So you know what I did? I got all dressed up and I marched down there to see my daughter. I rang the bell and that snotty woman, Richard's mother, opened the door. The lint in her pocket probably cost more than everything I had on. She looked down at me and raised her eyebrows so high.

"I come for my grandchild's birthday celebration," I said.

"You're not on the list," she answered.

"What list? I don't need a got damned list. Where's my daughter? I want to see her right now!" I screamed.

"Pearl doesn't live here anymore," the woman said.

"Where's the baby?"

"He's here, where she left him. Can't say I didn't warn my son. Now we have this *mess* on our hands. You make sure you tell that daughter of yours that it's too late to come back."

The woman slammed the door in my face. And it was a good thing because I was about to hit her right on her fat nose.

How could they take Pearl's baby away? So you know what I did? I walked down the street then came back with a huge stone and I hurled it at the window. As soon as I did I could see Richard through the curtains, running down the stairs. He tore the door open and stormed out at me like a fire breathing dragon.

"What in the hell is wrong with you?"

"I wanna know where I can find my Pearl, and I want to see my grandchild!"

"Your *Pearl* is a whore!"

I was about ready to hit him square in the face. I pulled my fist back and squeezed my eyes together in a fit.

"She left a few months ago. When I see her she smells like liquor and God knows what else. She was here a couple of weeks ago and didn't come back with my son until three in the morning. I told her she couldn't leave with him again. It was the last time I saw her. And hopefully I won't be seeing her again after this. She stays down there on Oak street."

"What did you do to run her away from here? From her own home?"

"Nothing. She left because she wanted to."

I walked away from Richard. I was flabbergasted! My Pearl, lied to her own mother? Richard said she lived on Oak Street. Oak Street? In the ghetto? Why? Why was my baby doing this? Leaving her own child? Gone? Where was she getting the money to help with my mortgage?

What happened? Was she gonna help me with the mortgage!? What about my bills?

I drove down to Oak Street. I drove down to Oak Street every day until I saw her. She looked cheap. Her clothes were tattered and her shoes had holes in them. What did she do with the beautiful clothes Richard bought her? My goodness I must convince her to go back. Beg. Cry. Crawl. Grovel if she must! I stopped the car! I got out. I threw my arms around her. She stunk. Wreaked of something, just like Richard said. "Why?" I asked.

She shirked my arms from around her and put some bills in my hand. I shoved them into my purse and followed her to where she lived, in an abandoned building. Again I asked, *"Why?"*

Then she said, "It don't matter."

I followed her up the stairs to a little dirty room. There was a man waiting for her when we got there. She walked over to him and lay across his lap right in front of me! The nerve, the disrespect. What was going on with *my* Pearl?

"Surely this isn't the life you want to live?" I asked.

"Why not? I've been living a life I didn't want my entire life. Richard was the man *you* wanted to marry. He wasn't the one I wanted. And I didn't want to bring no babies into this screwed up world either. That was *your* plan. Did you think they was gonna like me? Or care about me just cause I had his child? Well guess what? They didn't care. All they wanted to do was take him away from me. But they didn't have to cause I didn't want him anyway. I didn't want that LIFE, that MAN, that BABY, their MONEY, or that EMPTY HOUSE. Least now I get to choose the life I don't want."

Pearl took out a little plastic bag with some white stuff in it. Her man friend pulled out a tiny mirror and a straw. Then she dumped the contents on a compact mirror that she had taken out of her purse...right in front of me. Her friend gave her a razor blade and together they lined the powder up.

Pearl and her friend pulled the straw to their noses, then started sniffing the white powder. I just stood there, looking at her. Flabbergasted! I smacked it out of her hand. Suddenly, Pearl jumped up and lunged at me like a deranged lunatic. So I smeared the powder across the floor with my foot, leaving the imprint of my shoe in the powdery dust. Pearl slid to her knees with the straw in her hand and started sniffing the white powder right from the floor. The both of them.

"Why?" I asked again.

She looked up at me, sniffling...

"I was bored stiff mama. (SNORT!) Rich folks do stuff they ain't suppose to do too. Where you think I learned how to do this?"

She looked at me for a moment, her eyes never wavering then said, "Don't come back no more! I don't want you to see me like this! Go!"

She got off the floor and started throwing stuff around the room. So I did what any sane person would do in middle of something crazy, I ran. And I ran. No sense could be made of what happened to my Pearl. I felt hurt, shocked, and betrayed. I needed somebody to talk to. So I ran home. And when I got home, I waited for husband. But, I didn't have a husband no more. I was alone. Completely alone. I don't have to tell you what happened next....

I couldn't afford my house no more. And I could barely eat. I didn't have nobody. No husband. No grandchild. No daughter, whom I passed on the streets sometimes. I don't look at her, she don't look at me. She just be standing on the corner, laughing with them street hustlers, faking happiness, looking high. I ain't got nothing at all... no friends, no family and no money! I sat in my house staring at the walls. Daydreaming. Wishing there was something like a roast in the oven instead of noodles in the pot. I didn't have no retirement money. Didn't work as much as I was supposed to. All I had was my social security check. And that wasn't enough! I sure wished I had what I had before all that stuff happened. My husband. My daughter. Something, anything to remind me of yesterday. When I was truly rich, or what some people call *blessed!*

I sat in my kitchen waiting. Waiting for my eggs to finish cooking. All I had to eat was some eggs and canned ham. Or so I thought. The doorbell rang. I opened the door. A handsome young man was on the outside. I knew him from somewhere. He was so handsome and clean he was glowing. I thought the angels had come for me.

"Good morning, Ma'am. It's nice to see you again."

I gave him a funny look.

"I don't mean to disturb you. I was walking by when I saw smoke coming out of your windows. Is everything all right?"

He looked over my shoulder at the empty frying pan burning on the stove top. I smiled, because I recognized his face.

"Boy? Is that you?" I squinted my eyes. "It's so nice to see you. It's so nice to see somebody. Come on in."

"I can't."

He looked at my face thoughtfully, for a moment. "Well maybe just for a minute... so how's Pearl?" He walked over to the couch. We sat.

"She fine, baby. She got everything she ever wanted. Looks like life's been good to you boy."

"Well, I can't complain. Just got out of college a couple of years ago. Got a good job. Making good money too."

My heart lifted.

"*MAYBE* you could go see my *ANNA*. She always liked you...always."

"—I'm married now." The boy stood up and looked at me, his eyes filled with sadness, empathy, and something else. He then reached into his pocket and took out some bills that he stuffed into my hand.

"Hey breakfast is on me this morning. Maybe we could go together some time. You can tell me how Pearl's doing."

I couldn't look at him. So I don't say nothing. Let alone, I couldn't hear him no more. He, who looked for a moment like my last hope. And I don't remember him walking out the door either. So I sat there, with my eyes closed feeling like there was nothing left in the world to look forward to.

I was tired. Cold. Hungry. Lonely. And po'. So tired, that I laid down with my fingers clutched around them dollar bills the boy put in my hand. It was all I could do. Thinking last of my Pearl and my husband, I closed my eyes. I **COULDN'T** open them no more. I didn't **WANT** to open them no more. So I didn't... and days later when the neighbors found my cold, brownish blue body on the couch, they pried them bills from my hand.

When you laying beneath the cold, moist soil of the ground after having spent a lifetime lusting and desiring for things that don't mean nothing. You just may end up exiting the gates of life with nothing in your pockets but a broken heart. I guess in the end it's when you realize *that you can't take it with you.*

About the Author

E. Hughes is the author of novels, *Sixth Iteration, Disappear, Love, Infatuation, A Mediterranean Romance: The Capa Royals, Business as Usual, and The Sapphire Chronicles*. She is also a poet and author of the poetry book, *Beyond the Plain* and philosophy book, *Time and the Multi-Universe: A philosophy of time and time travel*. She is also the author of children's books, *Penelope: Be Kind to Animals, Penelope: Helps Mom and Dad, and Penelope: Super Duper Spectacular Princess Ballerina*, Penelope: Holiday Cheer and Penelope: Don't be afraid.

Hughes is a screenwriter with over twenty years of writing and publishing experience. She has taught publishing for five years, and has served as president of a national publishing company bringing hundreds of book to the market. She has appeared in films as a voice actress, and has directed a featured length independent animated movie. She is also an artist, recreational gardener, and a hobbyist jewelry designer.

9 781961 823037